My Sister's Silent World

Words by Catherine Arthur

Pictures by Nathan Talbot

 CHILDRENS PRESS, CHICAGO

    3 4 5 6 7 8 9 10 11 12 R 85 84 83 82 81 80 79

Library of Congress Cataloging in Publication Data

Arthur, Catherine.
  My sister's silent world.

    SUMMARY: A child describes her sister's hearing
problem and the family's birthday visit to the zoo.
    [1. Deaf—Fiction. 2. Brothers and sisters—
Fiction] I. Talbot, Nathan. II. Title.
PZ7.A74359My   [E]   78-13140
ISBN 0-516-02022-6

My Sister's Silent World

Today is my sister Heather's birthday.
She's eight years old. Mom and Dad said
Heather can decide what we will do today.

Heather wants to spend the day at the zoo.
That's her favorite place.

At the zoo we can watch the animals play. We can see them being fed. And sometimes we can even touch the animals. But Heather doesn't hear the sounds that the animals make. Heather is deaf.

You can't tell by looking at someone that they are deaf. Being deaf isn't like catching a cold or having the measles. There aren't any red spots. And being deaf doesn't make you sneeze. And it doesn't go away.

Heather can hear some noises. When we are at the zoo, an airplane flies overhead. The noise makes me cover my ears. But the noise isn't loud to Heather. She can hear the plane. But she can't tell which direction the noise is coming from.

With a hearing aid, Heather can hear some sounds when people are talking. But she can't hear the words. A hearing aid makes sounds louder so Heather can hear more than she can without it.

Learning how to talk is hard for Heather.

I help her learn new words. To understand what I say, Heather has to look at me when I talk.

She watches the way my mouth, face, and tongue move. She puts her hand on my throat. Heather can feel the way my throat moves. When she tries to say the word, she puts her other hand on her own throat. Heather tries to make her lips and face move the same way mine do.

Heather asks me the names of the different animals at the zoo. She uses her hands to talk to me. When she makes signs with her hands, she is saying different words and letters. I know how to use sign language too. Sometimes we make up new signs that no one else understands. That's our own special code.

Heather learned to talk with her hands at a special school. School is fun for Heather. She learns how to do the same things that kids around her do. She is learning how to read and write and talk better.

Sometimes people act funny when they hear Heather talk. She doesn't always get the words to sound right. Sometimes they laugh and call her names. They think she can't understand what they are saying. Sometimes they won't even look at her.

Sometimes it is hard for other kids to understand Heather. At first, they are afraid to play with her. They think they will have to be careful of Heather because she is deaf. They think it will be hard to be her friend.

But Heather likes to do the same things that other kids like to do. She likes to ride her bike, play baseball, and go to movies.

We are all hungry for birthday cake and ice cream when we come home from the zoo.

We sing "Happy Birthday" to Heather.
She understands. We can tell by her smile.

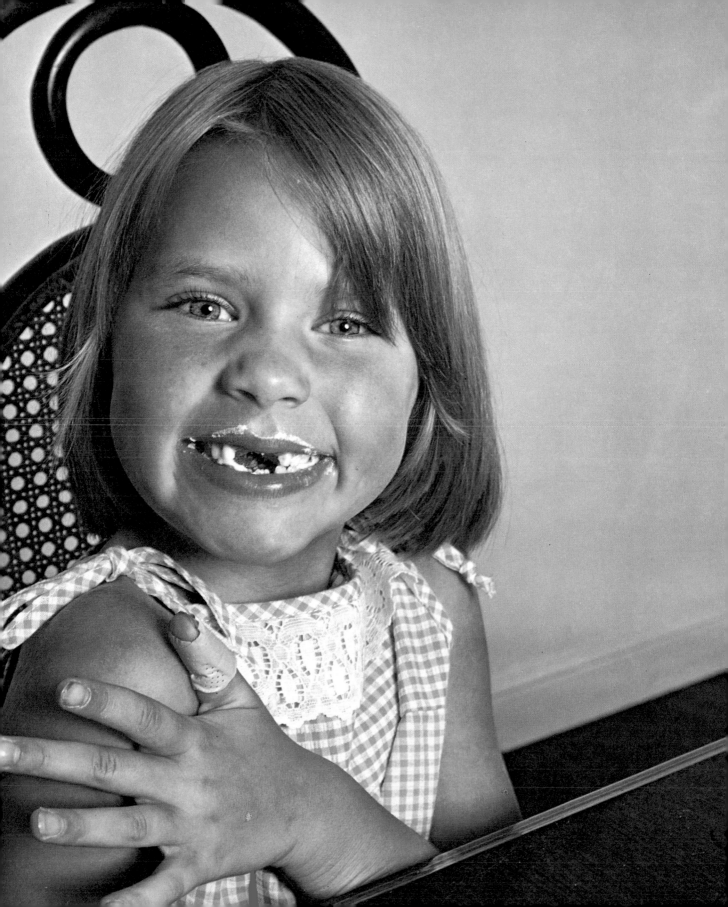